Grandpa's Our Hero

By Marisa Kristine Hernandez

This book is dedicated to my grandpa David Hernandez,
who was the best grandpa anyone could ask for and always made
sure family was most important.

My grandpa has been there since the beginning that I could remember.

He picked me up from school and we got paletas in spring, summer and September.

We would always play tea pot while he
wore his cowboy hat
and we would watch the sunset on the
porch where we sat.

Sometimes we would play Goldfish:
"Do you have any Ace's, two's or
Queen's?"
and he would say no, but secretly
have all three.

We would eat all the pizza at the Golden Corral
And my cousins and I would have sleepovers: "Build tents, we shall!"

When grandma saw what we did with her blankets
she got in a fit
but grandpa came to save the day.
"Come on kids, show us your skit!"

He was the life of the party
He loved to dance
He did The Twist
At every chance.

He danced with all his grandkids
La Bamba too,
but this he danced with grandma
and the family cheered, "woo hoo!"

Coaching basketball was his game
He loved watching it and always came.

As we all got older, so did he.

He knew every referee.

I saw him applaud and cheer

As he always sat near.

I would stop by grandpa's to say hello
And he would say "Whoa, you've grown!"
We ate tamales and arroz con leche
Until it was time to get up to stretch.

Grandma loved to gossip

And was happy to show me clothes from her closet.

He sat on his favorite chair

While grandma tried to sell her clothes in a pair.

I kept growing up and so did he.
He always called and talked with glee.

Now living in New York, he would call
to say,
"Family is important, please don't
stray."

Being a superhero was his thing

He always bounced back in full swing

He was still funny grandpa but something happened

He got very sick
And grandma and her children came running quick.
Everyone prayed and was shaken
But we knew he was in good hands to be taken in

Grandpa will be watching over us with his plan
Because he was our biggest fan.

Grandpa David is now gone

But his family will cherish the memories until dawn.

Remembering his jokes, keeping his faith alive

Because don't forget he had five

To remind the next generation that family is important,

And happiness with family can't be shortened.

About the Author

Marisa Kristine Hernandez is a Mexican-American actress, model, producer, and author born and raised in San Antonio, Texas. In the fall of 2016, Marisa moved to New York City to pursue her acting career. Since then, Marisa has walked in NYFW, starred in short films, and is currently creating her own work. She loves to spend her free time with family and by watching TV. She lives in New York City.

CPSIA information can be obtained
at www.ICGtesting.com
Printed in the USA
LVRC010333120421
684207LV00012B/196